MARIA

ALWAYS AVAILABLE

RICHARD LEE

*Dedicated to a world in need of
love and imagination.*

"He who hesitates is a damned fool." - Mae West

CONTENTS

FOREWORD

The EROS CRESCENT novels - *The Fifi Code, Eros Crescent* and *Mount Eros* - take you on a journey like no other - to places you couldn't imagine - a female friendly sex club or a privately owned members-only dogging venue; the toy-boy life of a writer working on the Amalfi coast and much much more. *MARIA* and the other novellas - *JANICE, JESSICA, HELEN, MARY* and *THE CLUB* - are extracts taken from *The Fifi Code, Eros Crescent* and *Mount Eros*. All are available as Kindle ebooks or as paperbacks at Amazon.com

PREFACE

As interactions go, what happened the next morning was most unexpected. Roger's deep sleep was only slightly disturbed; so slight as to allow him to offer no visible indication that he was awake or aware of what was happening.

Roger's head lay to the side pointing in the direction of the door and, also, the enchantress with her head beneath the sheets. He decided to open one eye just a tiny amount to see what might be visible to him.

– *from Eros Crescent*

1

_____

MARIA

It was during his first weekend in the new house in Eros Crescent that there was a knock on the door at mid-morning. Roger was making coffee in the kitchen and wondered who it could be. Who would know he was there?

A smiling woman dressed all in black and with a full figure beamed at him when he opened the door.

Hello. I'm Maria and I live over the back, on the far side of the bush park with my daughter Serina. I should mention that we had the job care-taking your house for the few months before you arrived, so we both know your house very well.

"We clean and cook for people in the area. I was wondering if you might be looking for someone to help in the house. I heard you were on your own and so thought it wouldn't hurt to call and ask. I'm happy to work just one day a week, or more if you wish."

She stopped talking and handed Roger a piece of paper with her name and phone number.

"Well, Maria. It's lovely to meet you and you're right. I will need someone just to vacuum and keep the kitchen tidy. And I'm prepared to hire you for a day a week right now. Choose your day and hours. I'm Roger Robertson by the way"

Maria smiled and Roger noticed that beautiful thing he so often saw in older women that he could never properly describe. He put her age at around fifty but with that lovely healthy southern European skin colour it was difficult to know.

"You certainly make up your mind quickly, Mr Robertson. Well, how about Tuesdays starting at nine and finishing at two? Is that okay?"

"Sounds good to me. Here, I'm sorry, do come in Maria and look around in case you have questions."

"It's a big house, Maria, as you must already know, but I'm only using the kitchen, the lounge and a bedroom and bathroom upstairs. The rest of the house is not used, so don't worry about cleaning it. Eventually, when my sister arrives later in the year, she and her partner will occupy the house and I will move into the cottage at the back."

"It all looks good to me, Mr Robertson. Will I start next Tuesday?"

Maria wandered around the kitchen as she spoke and Roger couldn't help noticing her curvy body in her tight black short skirt and skivvy and stockings.

"Yes, Maria, that would be good. Oh! I should tell you that I mostly work at night, so you might not always see me until late in the morning or even the early afternoon. Because of that, I will give you a key and I will leave your money in the cutlery drawer in an envelope. Now how much should I leave?"

***

Roger usually worked late on Monday nights, so rising early was not something he ever did on a Tuesday. It was a habit he'd acquired when working as a night watchman to provide a little income while waiting for the first decent royalty payment from his first novel, published two years earlier.

With bedtime usually around 2 or 3 am, nothing could wake him until around ten or eleven, but glancing at his diary late at night, Roger saw that Maria would be coming in to work for the first time the next morning at nine o'clock, so he took the precaution of closing the bedroom door in anticipation of the sounds of the vacuum cleaner and the laundry equipment.

Roger had warned Maria of his sleeping habits but didn't want her feeling that she had to creep around trying not to wake him. And she knew that money had been left for her in an envelope on the kitchen dresser, so it wasn't necessary for him to speak with her before she left at around two o'clock.

With the above arrangements in place, Roger felt secure in falling asleep without any concern for the domestic matters of the day. Oblivion would be easy and he would wake up to a clean house and clean washing. So it was something of a mystery to him later when he awoke and found that he was able to recall an incident that had happened earlier.

Roger could only guess that it had occurred quite early in the morning. He was aware that the bedroom door had opened and someone had come and stood beside the bed, seemingly to look at him in repose. He was not cognisant enough to open his eyes or move in any way, but on reflection he remembered a faint smell of perfume.

The person, whom Roger realised could only be the new home help, had then retreated, closing the door softly as she went.

So what was it that had brought her into the bedroom? Was there something she had considered required his urgent attention but then, on seeing him fast asleep, she changed her mind?

It would remain a minor mystery for now, but it did get Roger thinking that he could not have a home help whom he never saw. It might seem all right to have a magic genie fix the house while he was asleep, but he could see that Maria might have regular questions and enjoy some contact with him.

Roger resolved to set an alarm for ten thirty next Tuesday morning and to make an effort to become a more sociably responsible employer.

The following Monday night, Roger got to bed a little earlier and set the alarm. He would rise and shower and dress and be down for breakfast at around ten forty-five. He would be able to be a sociable person and available for any domestic matters or other things that Maria might like to talk to him about. It would also give him an opportunity to ask questions about the area where he was now living and perhaps learn something about his neighbours.

It would be good for him, he mused. Maria was an attractive woman, and seemed a very likeable person, and also, in his rush into the writing of this new novel, Roger ran the risk of returning to a habit of spending too much time alone.

Certainly, one needed peace and quiet, but equally one benefited from contact with people, however simple these interactions might be.

As interactions go, what happened the next morning was most unexpected. Roger's deep sleep was only slightly disturbed; so slight as to allow him to offer no visible indication that he was awake or aware of what was happening.

Gentle fingers wrapped themselves around his shaft and moved up slowly until they reached just below the crown, and it was as much as he could do not to quiver or shake as a soft mouth enclosed the top and a tongue slid around below his knob and then went back to the top and lapped at his urethra, likely finding a small night emission.

Roger's head lay to the side pointing in the direction of the door and, also, the enchantress with her head beneath the sheets. He decided to open one eye just a tiny amount to see what might be visible to him.

There, within inches of his face was a large shapely backside sheathed in a tight black skirt, which had pulled itself upward as the wearer had arranged herself on the bed.

Roger had not failed to notice her more than adequate posterior when he had first met Maria, but her beautiful smile and youthful countenance and remarkable shining eyes, not to mention her sufficiently partially uncovered bountiful chest, had probably got to him first. He remembered thinking that this widow must surely have many admirers.

Not wanting to move his head for fear of disturbing her, Roger let his eyes travel as far as they could along her body. Where her skirt ended, the end of a suspender peeped over the smooth white skin of her thigh and clasped the top of a black stocking, which then ran smoothly down her leg to a smallish foot and a low-heeled black shoe.

Suddenly the mouth gave a long but gentle suck as it dragged itself up Roger's shaft and away from his member. Then Maria removed her head from the bed, rolled gently over, got up and left, softly closing the door behind her.

Roger lay without moving, not wanting to lose these recent thoughts and sensations. But then he was forced to wake up to address this extraordinary event, turning it over and over in his still dazed mind.

This amazing woman had had her way with him secretly, or so she thought, and for now Roger would give no hint to his lovely visitor that he knew about it.

Maria had accepted Roger's offer of accommodation in the empty cottage adjoining the house within a day of the violent storm that had swept across the city, dropping a giant tree on Maria's house.

When the final furniture and essential household stuff had been delivered, along with Maria's daughter Serina and Maria's late husband's elderly father, Alberto, and Maria's boarder, Giorgio, the newly arrived distant relative of Alberto, Roger welcomed them all and told them they could use the kitchen and lounge in the main house if they felt a bit cramped.

Maria's daughter Serina knocked on the study door early one afternoon, just a couple of days after the family had moved into the cottage. Roger called "Come in". He thought that it would be Maria.

"Hello Serina. Nice to see you. Don't know that you've ever been into my writing room. There is not much to see, but what is here does the job. Is this just a social call Serina or was there something you wanted to ask me? Is everything all right in the cottage? That easy chair might be better to sit on. Sitting on the chair opposite me and the desk feels sort of formal, doesn't it?"

Serina took the seat. She was dressed neatly in a skirt and blouse and little shoes. At their first meeting he found her a little unnerving. He figured that she was somewhere in her late twenties or early thirties. He knew that she had been married briefly because Maria had mentioned it.

"I just thought I should ask if everything was all right, Roger?"

Roger noted that the question sort of inferred that things might not be all right. "Why yes, Serina. All is well. I assume you're thinking about your mother and her working here one day a week. If that is the case, yes, all is fine so far as I am aware. Should I be concerned? Have I maybe offended her? What are you thinking, Serina?"

There was a long pause and Serina actually stopped staring at him for the first time and gazed out of the window instead.

"I know she still misses Dad."

Roger relaxed back into his chair, relieved that this was not about him.

"He died nearly four years ago and Mum hasn't shown any interest in any other men since then. They had a strange married life in some ways. Over the last twenty years or so Dad worked night shift, getting home at around 3 am and sleeping until midday. Mum worked at a shipping company cafeteria and left home around 7.30 each morning. They spent very little time together."

Real-life stories were of particular interest to Roger as a writer. They helped provide background and substance to his work, often just in small unrelated ways.

"When I was around fourteen or fifteen, I would often find it difficult to sleep and would wake up and go and get into bed just before dawn, beside Mum. She always felt so warm and reassuring and welcomed her little girl with a hug and a kiss.

"I began waking up most mornings in their bed. Dad never really knew I was there. I would be well and truly gone when he woke up.

"It was then that I discovered something unusual about my mother. Most times I'd wake up as mum left the bed to go to work.

Occasionally, when I felt her body moving, I would become semiconscious and aware of her movements."

"One morning, I was sufficiently awake to notice mum moving in the bed. Usually, when this happened I would just doze off. But this morning I didn't and to my surprise, I discovered that mum was very gently sucking my dad's cock. Then after a short time she simply left the bed and headed off for breakfast and work.

"From then on, I observed her doing this on most mornings. It seemed that my father never knew what was going on and she obviously didn't want to wake him."

Roger stared at her in disbelief. Could this be a clue to what was happening to him, early on Tuesday mornings?

"I worked out that Mum and Dad were almost totally separated by their shift work and so rarely, if ever, had the opportunity to be sexually active. It appeared that mum had discovered a way of satisfying herself, at least partially, and it seemed like it was working for her."

Roger looked closely at Serina. She seemed to be totally absorbed in her story.

"After Dad died, life went on pretty much as usual. I still climbed into Mum's bed in the early mornings and cuddled up to her.

"One morning, only a short time after Mum had left the bed, I remembered I needed to work on something before school, a test or something, so I got up.

"Mum wasn't in the kitchen and I wondered where she was. Then, as I walked barefoot to the bathroom, I noticed that grandpa's bedroom door was open. I glanced in and couldn't believe what I saw. There was Mum with her head moving up and down under the duvet sucking on my sleeping Gramps' cock."

Roger was still staring at Serina, trying to take in all that she was telling him.

"And your grandpa? He didn't wake up either?"

Serina smiled.

"Grandpa usually watches television until late, then reads Italian newspapers, drinking his vino and laughing and calling out things in Italian. "In vino veritas" was his catch phrase. You would never see

Grandpa up and about until late in the mornings; and he slept like a log."

Serena paused, staring out the window and obviously reminiscing.

Roger took advantage of this moment of silence to order his thoughts. Why was Serina telling him all of this? Did she know something about what was happening on Tuesdays? Was she warning him of something he hadn't thought of?

"So Serina? How does this affect me and why are you telling me?"

Serena turned from staring out of the window.

"There is something I haven't told you, Mr Robertson, sorry, Roger. It would seem that what happens when mum starts her day in the early morning, is that she is likely to visit you. She may have already, but you don't know about it. Now that we are living in the cottage and with easy access to your house, I'm thinking that you will almost certainly have an early morning visitor."

Roger was silent. Should he tell Serena that this had already happened? But then he had only discovered it by accident really, and Maria didn't know that he knew. Keeping quiet seemed the better option.

"There is one more thing, Roger. One day, not long after I discovered what Mum was doing to Dad before she left the bed, I put my hand out immediately she'd left and took Dad's cock in my hand. Moments later, I had my mouth over it, doing what Mum did. Then I stopped and ran to my room and masturbated. From then on, it was a regular thing that I did. That early sexual experience remained with me and with Dad gone, I missed it desperately.

"My mother and I now share this sexual affliction, if one can call it that. Living in the cottage right next door to you, Roger, and you sleeping late as you do, it's going to be hard, not just for Mum but for me too, not to visit you early in the mornings."

Roger was in awe of this beautiful young woman. He was also speechless. As he began to formulate a response, Serina rose slowly from her chair.

"Thank you, Roger. I better not keep you from your work any longer. Thanks for listening. I hope I haven't frightened you?"

Serina turned and smiled an appreciative smile.

"You are such an attractive man Roger. Please don't lock your doors at night. Getting through windows is something neither I or my mother are good at."

Serena gave a wicked laugh and smiled.

"Oh yes, there is one other thing, Roger. Mum knows about me just as I know about her. We support each other. We are very happy to either share, or take turns. Thanks, Roger. See you soon."

Serena glided majestically from the room and Roger slumped back in his swivel chair, his thoughts wildly trying to order themselves properly.

One question kept bobbing along in the background. How would Maria or Serina respond if Roger simply woke up and wanted to fuck one or the other? Or both of them?

It was Maria's cleaning day and Roger made sure he was up and shaved and dressed and presentable before heading downstairs for his first coffee of the day.

As usual, Maria was looking attractive and Roger appreciated both her looks and her energy.

For the umpteenth time, Roger thought about if and when he would make it known to Maria that he knew about her secret Tuesday morning visits to his bed when he was in a deep sleep and how much he enjoyed her gentle sucking his cock before quietly leaving, well before he awoke.

He was ready to confront Maria and even attempt to seduce her but when he said her name as she folded clean tea towels on the kitchen table, Maria got in first.

"Roger, I have one thing to tell you and one thing to ask you. Is now a good time?"

Maria's smile was irresistible and Roger indicated that he wanted to hear what she wanted to tell him. He assumed that they would be about the house and working. He was in for a shock.

"Please! No time like the present as they say in cheap novels."

Maria fixed him with a look that foretold that a secret was about to be divulged.

"As you know, I do housework and sometimes cooking for a number of wealthy clients here in the Western suburbs. One of my customers is a woman named Desley who is the daughter of the long dead but well known brothel keeper, Kathleen Mary Leigh. Kathleen Leigh famously bought the house near by and she was instrumental in naming this crescent Eros Crescent. Mount Eros is the name of their house; number thirteen, on the other side of the track leading up the mountain."

Roger smiled and said how he knew the name and had read the inscription on the plaque at the edge of the park.

"Well, a couple of months ago, Desley opened a club. She runs a charity for older and out of work prostitutes, so she thought what better way to raise money than exploiting an activity she knows a lot about. She has slowly built the reputation of the club so that now it is so popular, she has been forced to limit membership and stop accepting new enrolments, unless of course, another member leaves. But she now has plans to open a second club on the other side of the harbour, probably at Neutral Bay or somewhere on that side of the harbour bridge, anyway."

Roger put up his hand.

"Before you go on, Maria, just fill me in on what is special about The Club?"

Maria laughed and for a moment Roger thought he saw her blush.

"It's basically a sex club. It shows end-to-end blue movies for the six hours it is open on six days of the week. But before you say that it sounds sordid or creepy, I should tell you more about it.

"Desley went to a lot of effort to set the place up. It is beautifully designed and very functional. But what makes it unique is that it is female friendly. She thinks it is the first of its kind and she thinks she will eventually be able to sell the concept around the world.

This leads me to why I'm telling you about it. Desley is looking for a person to write up the story of The Club and what she has achieved. She wants something in print that properly describes the club, the way it functions and how it is used. She also wants something that can be used as a prospectus for likely overseas clients.

I told her that I thought I knew someone who would be good for the job and who might be interested. I lent her a copy of your previous book and she loved it and enthusiastically said she wanted to meet you.

Roger looked at Maria intently, digesting what she was telling him. His first reaction was of disbelief that such a place could exist.

"I've visited sex shop movie theatres in New York and in Amsterdam. I can't see how they could possibly be restructured to provide enticing entertainment for anyone other than the most desperate people, mostly male and very rarely, female.

Have you been to the club Maria? And if so, what was it like? From a woman's point of view."

Roger watched as Maria coloured up again.

"Well, yes I have, Roger. I have long enjoyed an active sex life, both with men and with women and Desley knows that. Desley gave me a free membership to The Club and I can only report that so far, I've loved it. It does it for me and from what I observe, it does it for all the other women I see there. And the men seem very happy too."

Roger was in a sort of shock. The sad pervy men attempting to grope the unattractive and equally sad women who he had observed in adult theatres overseas could never fit with what Maria was telling him.

"Desley said she would be happy to pay a considerable sum of money for the story and hoped I would be able to interest you in the project.

"There is one other thing though, before you meet her. I am allowed to take a visitor to the club. It's all part of the membership. Three visitor tickets a year. She insists that I take you along to see the place working prior to her meeting you. She acknowledges that, having had that experience, you might not want to take on the job. I think she is right. You need to see it working.

"I suggest we go early one afternoon. You can accompany me and meet my friend Veronica. We mostly sit together. Then you can wander off and explore the club and we can see each other back here if we don't catch up at The Club at the end of the day. How does that sound, Roger?"

Roger was thinking fast. His natural interest in human behaviour was being teased out in a way that was hard to switch off. There was also an erotic component that could not be ignored. But his answer was swift.

"How could I not want to take up your offer, Maria? You might or might not have noticed that I have always acted appropriately in your company but I should put you on notice that this could change the instant we arrive at the club."

Maria laughed sympathetically and stared at him defiantly.

"Why would you wait until you were somewhere where there was likely to be stiff opposition, Roger? But perhaps a visit to The Club will encourage inappropriate behaviour in the future. We'll see."

Roger was immediately excited by Maria's suggestive stance. But he had questions.

"Maria? What would you say was the thing that made The Club experience so appealing to women? I can easily understand men being drawn towards interactions with women but I really do want to know what is the appeal for the ladies?"

Suddenly, Maria took on a different persona, showing an intellectual interest in what I had asked her.

"I'd put uncertainty and anticipation at the head of the list. The uncertainty coupled with the expectation and excitement of receiving unsolicited sexual attention, i.e., "Will someone I do not know, try to do something sexual to me when I wasn't expecting it?"

"The second thing, strangely enough, is the feeling of empowerment. A woman at The Club knows that ultimately she is safe but like all good stories, the opportunity is offered whereby the woman can suspend disbelief. She can pretend for just a short time, pretend that she will be surprised by titillating things that might happen to her, sexual things that she does not normally experience in her daily life.

"And thirdly, wanting to be adored is a natural trait of all women, even if it might be only temporarily. How much a man adores her is demonstrated by his persistence in wooing her despite the difficulties she might put in his way. She is in a position to reward or reject her would-be lover; or most likely, tease him and enjoy his tortured persistence.

"I love to have my boobs displayed and played with, but a man must work hard to persuade me before his fingers touch my nipples."

Roger eyed Maria and her bust, with more than intellectual appreciation.

"Tell me where to meet you and when, Maria, and I'll be there."

Maria smiled a wicked and beautiful smile. Then she reached forward and her hand closed over the bulge in Roger's pants. With her other hand, she unbuttoned her blouse exposing a low-cut bra.

"Bare my breasts Roger, please. I don't want to wait any longer. We've waited too long already."

A beautiful breast in each hand and a willing woman on the end of his penis while her legs waved wildly in the air, cleared all thoughts of anything else from Roger's head and he melted into the moment and between Maria's thighs.

This had been a long-time coming, and yes, he would tell Caroline, eventually.

Roger was very surprised to discover the location of The Club. Only a short walk from his own house and he'd never suspected that it was there.

He met Maria in what was originally intended as a car park, many years back, but which was now just a large flattened expanse of land that lay at the foot of the mount and stretched behind both numbers thirteen and eleven Eros Crescent.

Marie looked extraordinary. She was not wearing her usual black skirt and top but instead, a very short red miniskirt and a light cream coloured blouse with a frilly low neckline. Her bright red lipstick and her red high heels and white stockings pushed her appearance over the top. She took his hand and looked into Roger's eyes.

"Sorry about this outfit Roger, but it is the second Tuesday of the month. It's when Veronica and I meet two older lesbian ladies who we both happen to work for. They are super rich and live in big houses next door to each other in Vaucluse. They love to come over here once a month and have us together and wanting us to look as slutty as we can make ourselves without getting arrested. Interestingly, of the things that some women regret not doing in their younger days, dressing as sluts is one of them, although they will never admit it. If you sat close by and watched, you would be amazed at how many women approach us when we look like this. Far more interest from women than men."

Roger thanked Maria for her explanation saying that he was a little taken aback when he first saw her.

"I do hope today is going to work for you Roger. And can I say quickly, that when you wander off to see the sights, feel free to come back to me if I'm around. I will always be more than willing to bare myself to you. And Vickie will want you as well, I know what she likes. Mind you, though. today we might look just bit too slutty for your more refined taste."

Roger laughed and took Marie's hand and squeezed it.

"I just hope I can make myself ignore you both. Just for research purposes of course."

Marie burst out laughing.

"Now while I'm thinking about it, tell me about the films, Maria. The few I've seen in porn cinemas were often violent. How are the films here selected."

"Oh yes! I was going to mention that and then forgot. Desley's brother, Arnold has worked in the sex industry all his working life and is an authority on blue movies. He has selected an extensive range for viewing at the Club and all of them he and his sister have judged as female friendly or at least, close to. No rape or violence apart from the occasional bit of slap and tickle. The female club members seem to love them and can happily just sit and watch a movie with their skirts pulled up and their legs apart and their fingers busy. Seeing and watching them playing with themselves is one of the little known delights of being a member.

Alvie at the front desk even has a list of favourite movies that women clients would like to view again. Interestingly, the number one favourite is called Debt Collectors and depicts a woman being told by three gangsters that because her husband can't pay his debts, she will have to pay them for him, in kind. You can imagine what follows."

Roger stopped walking and took hold of the beautiful Maria and kissed her. When he thought he should stop, she wouldn't let him go and pressed her hand on his crotch.

"So looking this slutty hasn't put you off Roger. You must promise me that you will act inappropriately at your house whenever the idea enters your head. I will love it."

They were inside the door now and Roger looked around.

At reception, Maria flashed her membership card on the electronic reader and pointed to Roger.

"My guest, Alvie."

The older woman looked at Roger and smiled.

Alvie reached over and fastened a small tag to Roger's shirt showing the number 28.

"This must be your first visit? Haven't noticed you here before."

For just a moment, Roger felt like a naughty boy who'd been caught looking at a copy of a lad magazine.

"Yes! I'm looking forward to it."

"I'm sure you will enjoy yourself, love. Just remember the first rule, Slow and Gentle. That way no woman will ever disappoint you."

Maria beamed at Alvie and then at Roger.

"Let me know if you want to practice either or both of those things, Roger. Happy to give you a lesson if you think you need it."

Roger and Alvie laughed, enjoying Maria's innuendo. Alvie handed Roger a brochure entitled The Club Rules: Advice for New Members.

"Just in case you enjoy yourself so much that you decide to put your name down for membership, Roger.

Roger was impressed from the very beginning. The Club entrance area was bright and airy with white walls and brightly coloured doors and woodwork, and signage was clear and tasteful.

This small foyer area which led to the entrance to the cinema, was flanked by male and female bathrooms on either side, and signs pointed the way to two other venues. Signposts pointed to the Home Deliveries room and to Gals Only, and The Parlour seemed self-evident. Well, sort of. Roger had no trouble guessing the purpose of the Gals Only room but the Home Deliveries did not translate into something he could immediately identify and The Parlour, well that could be anything.

"Ready, Roger?"

Roger looked at Maria and smiled.

"Definitely ready, Maria."

It took only a few moments for Roger's eyes to adjust to the dim theatre lighting provided by the cinema screen. A movie played and provided gentle narration of a sexual encounter and with the voice of a woman screaming yes, yes, in the background.

The floor sloped down quite significantly allowing easy viewing over other patrons heads.

People were scattered around the theatre, some alone, some as couples and there was at least two sets of three people.

Maria pointed out to him that the three front rows were off limits to men unless they were with a consenting female partner. These front rows catered for couples and women on their own who did not want to be approached by other members.

Lone women would go there to simply watch the movie and likely touch themselves if so inclined. Occasionally - according to Maria - two women in a row might exchange glances and indicate that they would be happy to enjoy the other's company for mutual touching and kissing in which case, one or the other would get up and move next to her newly found friend.

Maria took Roger's hand and led him along one side to a row half-way down. Then she whispered, "Veronica will find us when she gets here shortly."

On the screen, two women were now laying on a bed kissing, each fully clothed but obviously interested in slowly removing bits of the others apparel. Close by, a semi-clothed man sat exposing himself on the bed and holding himself at the ready, awaiting the call.

Maria took Rogers hand and lent towards him and whispered. "Once your eyes have adjusted, feel free to wander off and check everything. I would suggest you start at the back wall where most men hang around while working out their next move and who they might approach. Your learning starts now, Roger. Best of luck."

Roger gave Maria a peck on the cheek then rose and turned to walk to the back.

When Maria called on Roger the morning after their visit to the Club, she announced that she had both bad news and some good news.

"Desley is away, overseas for three weeks, unfortunately, so she won't be able to see you yet."

Roger looked at Maria in her regular black outfit and found it difficult to remember her as the slut who took him to The Club the day before.

"And the good news?"

Maria bathed Roger with her most radiant smile.

"I can take you to the club again, but only if you want to go, Roger.

"Yes, Maria, I would love to be your guest again and yes I have a couple of questions. Well, probably a lot of questions but most can wait.

"The first one is probably obvious but I don't get it. What happens in the room labelled Home Deliveries. There are three doors, each named after a plant or flower, I think, but they were all locked. What happens in those rooms, Maria."

Maria's face looked a bit sheepish and she seemed uncertain how to answer, staring up to the ceiling while she formulated a reply.

"Ok! More and more of the female members are using the Home Deliveries booths although a number of members still don't really approve of it. There is a sort of stigma attached to the concept. It's seen by those members who consider themselves more superior, as a British working-class activity which is beyond the pale.

"Others have got over the shock and even if they don't yet use the rooms, they can appreciate the activity for those in need of it. By the way, those three booths are each named after a flower, Tulip, Buttercup and Primrose."

"Christ, Maria, for God's sake tell me what happens in the rooms. The suspense is driving me mad."

Maria giggled like a schoolgirl.

"Well, have you heard of dogging, Roger?"

Roger's mind took a sharp about face to accomodate what Maria had just said. Yes, he had heard of dogging.

"Are you serious, Maria? Do some members actually participate in this behaviour?"

"Oh yes, Roger, only the female members initiate it of course. But at the club, the activity is very different and we would never use the term dogging.

"Many women share the fantasy of being made love to - fucked, I suppose I should say - by more than one lover at the one time. The difference here is that the male suiters are club members and therefore "approved and certified" so to speak; not a load of stray smelly pervy types normally associated with dogging overseas.

"Not everyone uses the rooms, but more are enjoying it and dare I say that I can sort of understand why. We could perhaps discuss this at another time. Even I am a bit embarrassed thinking about it while talking to you. Sometimes in life you just do things, but which you don't talk about Roger, I'm sure you understand that, you being a writer and all.

"But now that you know what the rooms are for, let me tell you how it works.

"If a woman wishes to avail herself of Home Deliveries, she makes a booking at the office when she first arrives and she is allocated a time slot, usually a two hour period to allow time for getting things sorted, along with the name of her room. By the way, she also nominates her preferred number of delivery boys; two, three or a maximum of four.

"The arrival of swipe plastic key cards has made life much easier. Her booking time and details are logged into the system and a message is sent to her mobile approving her so that she can use her card as an access key. Her access, by the way, is via doors in the Gals Only room."

Roger continued staring at Maria.

"So how are men selected to become the lucky delivery boys?"

"Well, again, the computer and magic swipe card takes care of everything.

"Men who have checked in to The Club that day, receive a message on their phones telling them that a female member has made a booking at Home Deliveries for a certain time and in a particular room. A man simply needs to send back a Yes if he is interested. A half hour before the start time, men are advised whether or not they have been allocated a delivery slot by the system's algorithm and if they have, the room name and the time.

"There is more. When more than one woman has booked in, and there could be a number during the day given that there are three booths and quite a few two-hour slots, details of all bookings are sent out to checked-in male members.

"Many men will reply Yes to all of them, improving their chances of getting selected for one. They cannot attend more than one each day. The computer analyses the data and sends out a confirmation to those selected a half-hour before the event is due to begin. There is an option for the men to cancel if they suddenly find themselves other-wise occupied. This enables the computer to issue another person with an invitation and issue the first man with another invitation if another Home Delivery event is available.

"It has all worked very well, so far.

"Does that help, Roger? Any questions?"

Roger was staring at Maria in wonder. Then Maria smiled and answered the look on Rogers face.

"Oh yes, of course there is. Maria laughed, self-consciously, "And the answer is yes, Roger. Twice in fact, and I must say that on both occasions, it was just what I needed. I'm sure more women would do it if only they knew how cathartic it can be.

"Some women I've spoken to think that they need it most at certain times of the month. This might be true."

With his brain in overload, Roger managed to look into Maria's eyes.

"I want to come to The Club with you Maria. Can we go on a Tuesday? I liked Tuesday's at The Club."

Maria took Roger's hand and leant forward and kissed him gently on the lips.

"I love making love with you Roger. Make love to me and Veronica together, soon please. I'm sure you will enjoy a threesome. I know we would."

Roger laughed and slapped Maria lovingly on her rear.

"How could a man refuse two such elegant ladies."

"I think I should go to the kitchen and make us a sandwich, Roger. You've made me hungry."

Roger was excited about his second visit to The Club. It wasn't just the thought of having an opportunity to at last admit to himself that he was at heart, a voyeur.

As Roger and Maria walked towards the cinema door, Veronica arrived. Roger hadn't really met her properly last week and it was in the dark, so it was a surprise to meet a very slim small youthful looking woman in a very tight fitting skirt and top along with the obligatory stockings with seams, and high heeled shoes. In different clothing she could easily have passed for a university student.

"Pleased to meet you properly, Roger. Maria will try to keep us apart. Selfish bitch! But feel free to sit beside me any time you need a break from your activities. Smaller bites of someone special like me can be just what you need when the bigger girls on offer become over-whelming.

"And you can simply be with me and rest if you want. Just so long as you hold my hand."

Roger enjoyed the woman's wit and, looking at the grinning Maria, replied enthusiastically that he looked forward to such an opportunity.

Roger found Veronica's face especially appealing. While everything about her was fine and petite, Veronica's large brown googly eyes and her wide permanently open mouth displaying two rows of big bright white teeth framed by her huge stretched-out cupid lips was a siren calling from the shore.

Roger left Maria and Veronica and wandered up towards the back of the cinema. Looking around, he could see that things were starting to happen.

A couple of rows back, a man already had his hand inside a woman's wide open blouse and, without even glancing at him, she unbuttoned herself and lowered her bra to expose her nipples for him. At the same time, she wriggled her backside as she lifted her skirt and reached up and pulled down her knickers. At least, that's what Roger thought he would be seeing if he was closer. Bad light and his rampant imagination could well be robbing him of the true situation, but he didn't mind one bit. He decided to take a closer look.

Roger nodded goodbye to his two lovely companions.

"Don't get into trouble Roger. Come back here for that."

Roger moved leisurely up the aisle, noticing other things happening in almost every row.

In one row close by, two women had uncovered their breasts and each was busily licking and sucking the other. Both were in the act of lifting their legs and pulling up their skirts to provide each other with even greater access to the more intimate parts of their hungry bodies; and their mutual heavy breathing and gasping was audible and, Roger thought, strangely reassuring.

Roger reached the row of seats where the activity that had first drawn his attention was in progress. The couple occupied seats two and three leaving one seat at each end of the row, empty. Roger sat down beside the woman, who, sensing his arrival looked across at him and smiled. Then Roger felt her hand on his trousers and he knew he was now part of the game.

Roger lifted himself up and pushed his trousers and underpants down around his knees, letting his penis stand up, seemingly searching around in the dim light to discover its whereabouts. A hand came and took his hand and placed it on a breast and rubbed the breast with it gently. Then the woman's head turned and looked down at Roger's lap and she immediately reached out and took hold of his penis and began to rub it up and down lovingly.

The man on the other side, let go and raised himself to also drop his trousers and pants to his knees, exposing himself as Roger had done and almost immediately, the lovely lady took hold of him. Then she turned to Roger and leant towards him and whispered, "Kiss me like you love me."

Roger put his spare hand behind the woman's head and pulled her gently to him and kissed her, at first most softly but then, as she responded, the two mouths opened to each other and their passion burst forth.

"Oh, my God. Kiss me like that again."

The woman grasped Roger's penis with a stronger grip. Then she let go of the other man and pulled up her skirt to display a neat little tuft of pubic hair. Then she rubbed herself and in a hushed sexy voice said, "Tell me how much you want to fuck me. You do want to fuck me don't you? You want to very much I know. Say it!"

Roger had no difficulty telling her that fucking her beautiful pussy was the thing he most wanted to do in life which he honestly felt to be true at that moment. At that point, the woman had shuddered, leaving his mouth just long enough to groan before fastening her mouth back on his.

"Come and do it to me now. Put your beautiful cock in my cunt. And don't stop kissing me, you beautiful bastard."

Roger suddenly noticed that another woman had arrived and seated herself at the other end and in just moments she had stolen the other fellows cock and was unbuttoning her shirt and dragging his hand to her breasts.

"All's fair in love and war." Roger thought as he moved down between his lovers stockinged legs. He deliberated about what he would do and what she expected him to do. If she was wanting a cock inside her then cunnilingus was probably not where he should go right now. He slid his cock into her moist vagina and the woman wriggled around.

"Bang me hard my darling. And don't stop kissing me till I cum."

Roger decided that given how she was already hot and excited, he would exercise his usual cock hard in and then hold his end tightly up against her pubic bone, not letting her move away from it. If she was already in a state of excitement similar to what results from cunnilingus, then all should work out to both their satisfaction. And it did.

With their mouths still locked in a never ending kiss, the woman came and then came again. And when she thought she should move back to let him thrust, he wouldn't let her move, and to her great surprise and great happiness, she came again and then again and just kept coming and in the end Roger heard her final exclamation of a great outcry of "Oh Yes!".

Their kissing ended and the woman slumped back in her seat. She gasp and then spoke.

"Oh yes! You really loved me, didn't you, you sexy bastard. Promise you will find me again. My name is Jasmine and I'm here on Tuesday's and Wednesdays. Thank you. That was truly beautiful."

Jasmine rested her hand on Roger face and happily held his still monumental cock.

"You are beautiful Jasmine," replied Roger, purposely forgetting to offer his name. But then he noticed her looking at his visitor number.

"I will remember you number twenty-eight, and I will make sure that you and I go to heaven again. Thank you."

Roger sauntered back down to where Maria and Veronica where sitting, realising as he approached that the two women were not alone. What appeared to be the same two women that Roger had observed making love further up the aisle earlier, had now moved to be on their knees in front of Maria and Veronica. His friends lay back with their eyes closed and their lovely breasts on display. They held their beautiful legs up and wide apart and bent at the knees. Two heads were moving rhythmically between their legs, totally absorbed and slurping with great enthusiasm.

Veronica sensed Roger's presence and opened her eyes and looked up at him and smiled lazily.

"Show me your cock, Roger. I was just dreaming about you. Let me suck you."

Roger undid his belt and let his trousers drop to the floor and then he pushed down his underpants to join them. His cock was still rampant and Veronica's mouth dropped open.

"Oh Roger. You've been a naughty boy haven't you. Where has this been, I wonder. I can smell something nice. What a lucky lady; but she didn't finish you off, Roger?"

Veronica reached out and took Roger's cock in her hand.

"You distinctly told me, Veronica. Don't get into trouble. Come back here for that."

The two laughed, enjoying the gentle joke.

"Oh Roger, you are such a darling. May I finish you off now? I think I should before you get into any more trouble."

Maria opened her eyes and looked across at the two beside her, saw what they were doing and smiled.

"Oh you lucky slut, Veronica, he came back just for you. I'm very jealous."

Roger felt the small hand of Veronica and moments later, she opened her bright red lips and her mouth took charge. Her mouth movements were divine and it wasn't long before Roger erupted deep in her throat.

Veronica's big eyes smiled loving up at him as she gulped and then she held and lovingly licked his cock. As she did so, her flashing eyes moved back under her eyelids and her body stiffened and she gasped as the woman between her legs reached that certain point of no return. Veronica came and Maria came moments later, and the two ladies who had given them both such happiness, clasped each other and fell back on the floor, rubbing each other and calling out.

Veronica came out of her orgasmic trance and looked up at Roger.

"Promise me we'll do that again, Roger. I could happily suck your cock for ever. You are definitely the man I've been looking for."

———

When Maria arrived at Mary's house, she quickly assured Mary that she wasn't bringing bad news and that there was nothing wrong and that her visit was about things which were good and might help Mary.

"There are women like us, Mary, who just need to make love more often. Actually, I would put the number like us at around seventy-percent of women except many don't know and will probably never know what ails them.

"Staying healthy and happy demands that we live our lives fully and without too many restraints. I'm here because I believe I can offer you a solution; an answer to a horny woman's every fantasy."

Mary giggled and topped up Maria's coffee cup.

"Forgive me, Maria but you do sound as though you've taken on the local Tupperware agency. Should I be worried?"

Maria laughed. "Now that you mention, I do, don't I? But no, I'm here to tell you a story and you can tell me when I've finished, what you think. It will take a little while to tell, so please bear with me. But do interrupt at any time if you have a question.

Without saying where it was, Maria began to tell Mary about The Club.

"Imagine a place that is super safe, clean and well run and comfortable, where women can go to interact with men or women in order to enjoy a wide range of mutually agreed upon sexual exploits. I'm here to tell you that there is now such a place and I want to tell you about it.

Over the next forty minutes, Maria provided details of the organisation of The Club and the required code of behaviour. She thought it best to begin with what happens at the club because that was really what people want to know most and what Mary would be most interested in asking questions about.

And ask questions, she did.

By the time Maria had completed her discourse, Mary was truly excited. Maria asked Mary to repeat some of the things she'd told her just to be sure that she had understood the main points.

"So, Maria. I go to The Club and I'm wanting to meet a man, or as you've pointed out, maybe more than one man. I find a seat anywhere in rows six or seven, and settle back to watch the movie.

After just a short wait, a man will come and sit beside me and after a few minutes he will attempt to touch me, most likely on a leg or a breast or an arm. Then its up to me how I respond, encouraging him or discouraging him. If you want to make him work for his grope, refuse him a couple of times, three max, otherwise he will assume your not up for it. To get of rid of him, four rebuttals should do or just keep moving his hand away.

Meanwhile a second or even a third man might turn up and suddenly I've got more than I can safely handle."

Maria laughed at Mary's childlike enthusiasm.

"You've got it Mary."

"If I'm not getting any takers in six or seven, I can go and pick a shy bloke from rows four or five and do whatever I like with him.

"And if I want to meet up with a woman, I go and sit in rows eight and nine. In those rows we approach each other with signals - smiles and hand gestures. Sensitive touching and groping, and kissing and licking coming a few minutes later.

And if I'm with someone and we don't want to be interrupted by another horny person, we sit in rows ten, eleven or twelve. We also sit in those rows if we simply want to be alone and watch the movie and play with ourselves.

And finally, if I want to get ravaged, I go and park myself in row three where, in just a few moments I will be deluged with gropers and cock wavers prancing around in front and behind me.

The two woman laughed and Maria commented that she would love to make a movie of Mary on her first visit and how it could be hilarious.

"Now do you remember what other stuff is on offer, Mary?"

"Yep! Haven't forgotten a thing. The Gals Only room is where you can go with girlfriends to canoodle more comfortably, and you will also find dildo's there in two sizes. You can also have a wee and powder your nose. You can even use it as a bolt hole to escape from over zealous blokes.

"The Parlour is like the Gals Only room but it caters for both sex couples.

"Lastly, Home Deliveries sounds like the stand out! The sin-bin. Girls can make a booking and say how many blokes they would like to entertain. Allowable numbers are two, three and four."

"How am I doing, Maria, and where the bloody hell can I find this place?"

"Just tell me a couple of the rules Mary. I need to know that you know the rules."

"Easy, Maria, and number one, don't give anyone your name, phone number or address or any information that will allow them to find you anywhere other than at The Club.

"Arrive at The Club clean and properly clothed. I guess that means not covered in shit, and naked.

"Oh yes, important! Avoid getting into conversations. Talking is anathema to fulfilling your lustful desires. We all remember the visual hunk on sporting TV who made the mistake of trying to talk? And the same goes for women."

"So, my love. Just one more question. Would you like to come along as my guest next Tuesday afternoon. If you enjoy it, I'm allowed three visitor passes a year so that you can come with me again. So, Mary? Are you game? Can you face all those horny men and women?"

Mary's face became very serious as she murmured, "Yes please Maria. I would love that."

Mary's birthday party was drawing to a close. Most of the guests had said their farewells and wandered off.

Janice had shown great interest in Mary's new neighbours, in Number 21, Maria and her daughter Serina.

Helen - who was hosting the party - had been surprised and even a little shocked when she had bent down to pick up a spoon off the floor and looked under the table to discover that both Maria and her daughter each had a hand lovingly massaging the top of one of Janice's long legs, above her stocking tops and up and beneath the hem of her very short skirt.

So Janice hadn't changed much since her therapy with Helen the year before. She was obviously still addicted to sex, and sex from anywhere. What intrigued Helen was what Janice had done or said to initiate this reaction by the two women. They had obviously responded to something that she had told them.

Fancy that! Helen thought. Was it my pavlova that got them going?

She smiled inside, and when the three women rose to say good-night Helen could see by the smiles on their faces that they hadn't even started their real party yet. She suspected that the real excitement of the night was destined to begin when the trio arrived at Number 21.

When Janice and Maria and Serina left Mary's birthday party they held hands as they walked the few yards to the front gate of Number 21. The summer night was balmy, ideal for being outdoors.

Maria and Serina gently guided Janice along a winding path to a wide covered veranda. Instead of unlocking the door, the mother and daughter asked Janice to sit down on the comfy old sofa that sat against the wall. Then the two slowly gave in to their passions, starting by lifting Janice's legs into the air, removing her panties and taking turns in licking and sucking her cunt.

"Oh my goodness, what is happening? What are you doing to me," groaned Janice?

"Just say if you want us to stop Janice. We don't want to frighten you," Maria said quietly.

"Mum and I are hungry for you Sister Janice. Please don't worry. We won't hurt you."

But Janice loved it and lay back with just her hands fumbling in the darkness, surreptitiously seeking out the bodies of the two adoring women.

Janice smiled inside. At Mary's party, she had told Maria and Serina that she was only a week out of a convent and quite lost in this modern world. She said that she had become sexually frustrated and had fallen in love with another nun, who had rejected her and reported her to the Mother Superior.

She told Maria and Serina that she had been asked to leave. It had been suggested that she could join a teaching order and become a teacher and had been told to go away and think about it.

She finished her story by shedding a tear and dabbing her eyes and, within minutes, first Maria and then Serina put a hand on a thigh and caressed her above her stockings, whispering their desire to help her, and Janice knew she was on her way.

———————

Maria and Serina had both been boarders at convent schools and both girls had been mature for their age. As a result, both had enjoyed the sexual attention of nuns; so much so that, while Maria managed to remain a married woman, her daughter Serina found that the sexual life she shared with her husband was deficient and within a couple of years she found herself happily single again.

Now they enjoyed themselves in a variety of ways. Maria and Serina sometimes worked together as maids and kitchen hands for wealthy people, discovering that a few bored society ladies welcomed the opportunity to explore the bisexual aspect of themselves. A couple of these ladies regularly phoned and suggested it was time for one or both of them to pop over for coffee, cake and a little bit of fun. Sometimes they arranged to meet the two at a friend's beach house or some other location. One sometimes offered them her husband's cock, just for something a little different, and excitedly watched him fuck the two women in the french maids uniforms she made them wear.

When Maria and Serina did make visits, they took along sex toys in their bags and introduced their clients to a rich lesbian experience, although some of the woman they visited where able to teach Maria and her daughter a few things too.

They also enjoyed Grandpa Alberto, much to his appreciation. Alberto was blessed with good health and a very large and healthy cock, which both women were happy to handle lovingly. Nono Alberto slept a lot and spent much time outside in his garden.

Now they had Sister Janice, their new nun, just like the ones at school. With thoughts about their experiences with their attentive teachers, both wanted to devour Sister Janice as they had been taught to enjoy their teachers.

"Argh!" sighed Maria. "Sister Janice, you are beautiful. Say you will stay with us for a few days. Grandpa will love you as we do, and you will love him, especially his lovely cock."

Serina removed her mouth from Janice's and Janice whispered her response.

"That sounds wonderful, Maria. I'd love to spend time here, just so long as you both don't mind teaching me as much you can about sex and love. I want to make up for lost time and you are both so beautiful. And your Nono sounds exciting too. I've never seen a man's cock."

Janice was quite comfortable telling a lie or two as she moved her hand back between Maria's soft thighs and felt the wetness on her fingers. But Janice reminded herself once again that she must play the part of the innocent virgin nun who knew nothing about sex.

This masquerade she had thought up at Mary's party was already looking to be more exciting than she had imagined and Janice revelled in the idea that her two new ladies thought it was like having access to their misbehaving boarding school nuns from their younger days.

The delightfully lecherous Janice was intent on having every erotic stimulus that was on offer, and she would endeavour to satisfy herself and her new lovers in every way she could.

Janice awoke to the smell of fresh coffee. She felt very relaxed, probably from the fervent attention she had received the night before from her new lady friends. She leisurely touched herself between her legs, remembering the enthusiasm with which they welcomed her into their home.

Janice left the bedroom in search of coffee and something to eat.

"Good morning, Sister Janice! This is Father Munro. He's retired and totally deaf."

Janice had arrived in the kitchen to find Maria dressed in just a dressing gown and little Chinese slippers and standing at the stove making breakfast.

"There is muesli on the bench. Would you like bacon and eggs, or I can offer you toast with marmalade or strawberry jam? And how do you take your coffee?"

"A caffe latte would be good, Maria, and toast and marmalade please."

Janice looked at the elderly priest sitting at the breakfast bench. He was busy eating his bacon and eggs and didn't seem to notice Janice's arrival. He was a well-preserved older man, probably in his mid-seventies. Janice went and sat on a stool beside him.

Father Munro looked up and saw Janice smiling at him, he smiled back then continued eating. Maria came over with a coffee for the priest. Then she stood looking and smiling at Janice.

"Did you sleep well, Sister Janice? I hope you did. We did. I hope we didn't frighten you. Serina and I just couldn't get enough of you and we might have been a bit rough."

Janice looked back at Maria and fixed her with a gentle, loving smile, wishing she could blush on demand.

"Well, I did love it, Maria. And you were not too rough. I will look back on my first sexual encounter with the two of you as one of the luckiest and loveliest days of my life."

Maria came around the breakfast bar and put her arms out and Janice welcomed her with a loving hug. Then Janice asked Maria to kiss her and Maria did so with enthusiasm, while Janice slipped her hand inside Maria's dressing gown and caressed her breasts and felt her shudder.

"Stop it, darling. I don't want to stop, but there are things I must do. We will have time together later. I promise."

Maria smiled at Janice and moved back into the kitchen.

"Father Munro comes to visit once a month. We give him a little bit of attention, so to speak."

Maria threw Janice a knowing look.

"We enjoy it and so does he. But since we moved in here as caretakers, he hasn't been able to get an erection on any of his two visits so far. This is his third visit. I've played with it and put his hand between my legs, wriggled my bare backside in front of his face, but nothing seems to work. I don't know what more we can do, really."

Maria picked up a pencil and writing pad from the kitchen bench and started to write, speaking as she went.

"Because he's so deaf, I write him messages. I'm just letting him know who you are."

Then she took the pad and laid it beside Father Munro's plate for him to read and went back to making toast and coffee for Janice.

Janice thought for a moment and chose her words carefully. "Oh, how sad. I wonder if it's to do with your new accommodation? Maybe it just doesn't feel the same as your old place?"

Maria called back as she moved some things in the fridge.

"You could be right, Janice."

"Maria? If Father Munro hasn't got an erection, and I have never seen a penis, perhaps it would be a good opportunity for me to see his now so that I at least know what a limp one looks like. What do you think, Maria? Would it be improper for me to do that?"

Maria laughed. "You are so sweet, Sister Janice. Of course you can have a look. Have a feel too while you're there. His trousers are down around his ankles already. I'm sure he wouldn't mind."

Janice rejoiced in Maria's easygoing attitude and looked at the man sitting beside her. He was reading Maria's note. When he had finished it, he turned and looked at Janice and beamed a very big smile.

"Nice to meet you, Sister Janice," he said, holding out his hand.

Janice shook Father Munro's hand and smiled and mouthed a suitable reply.

"Nice to meet you too, Father".

So! He believed she was a nun too. What fun. Janice was intrigued. What was going on in the elderly priest's head? She was soon to find out.

Janice dismounted from the kitchen stool and squatted down beside the priest's hairy legs, and stared into the shadows. There, nestled in between his thighs was a mass of curly hair and, almost hidden in the middle and only just visible, she could see his shrivelled penis. Janice pretended to gasp.

"Oh my God! Maria! I can see it. I'm not sure what to do next. Please advise me, Maria."

"All right Sister Janice. Don't panic. Help is at hand. I'll be there in a moment."

Maria came around the bench and looked at Janice crouched down with her tight skirt pulled up and staring at Father Munro's cock. She also stared at Janice's divine legs and feet, knowing that she and Serina would feast on Sister Janice again later.

She lifted Janice's hand and placed it on top of the priest's cock and whispered.

"There, darling. Now just run your thumb and fingers over the top of it. You can also reach in underneath and find his balls and rub those. He loves having his balls rubbed. Now I'm just about to serve your toast and coffee, so don't be too long."

After just a few moments feeling the priest's genitals, Janice surfaced and sat back on her stool.

"Well, Maria! That was interesting. Thank you."

Maria replied, laughing.

"We'll find you an erect one later, darling. I think you will find that far more interesting."

Not long after Janice had started eating her toast and sipping her coffee, she felt a hand sliding up her stockinged leg, a strong hand that seemed to know where it was going. She said nothing. Janice let things stay as they were for a minute or two, enjoying the experience and wondering what Father Munro had in mind. Then a finger slipped into her panties and caressed her pussy. Janice thought she should respond with some encouragement, if only to be polite.

As Janice lifted her arm and hand from the table top and moved it down towards her leg, the priest's other hand came across and took hers and carried it across and wrapped her fingers around a very serviceable boner. A sharp thrill of surprise and pleasure ran through her genitals and Janice reminded herself once again that she must, under all circumstances, maintain her innocent persona.

"Maria?"

"Yes, darling? More toast?"

"Er, not now. There are things happening under the bench that you might need to come and help me with, Maria. Father Munro has got an erection."

Maria turned and stared at Janice. "Is that a joke, Janice?"

"No, it's not. He has just put my hand on it and I need your help please, Maria."

Maria walked over and round and looked at what was happening. She bent down and looked at Janice's hand on Father Munro's cock.

"Well, that is very interesting, Sister Janice. You obviously have the touch."

"Or maybe Father has a special interest in nuns?" replied Janice. "Did you say I was a nun on your note?" Janice reached out and pulled the writing pad over and read the words "Sister Janice".

"Yes I did. I think you might be right. So what would you like to do with it, Sister Janice? It's your call. I imagine that if I tried to take over, he might not appreciate it and lose his erection."

"I wonder what he did with other nuns, if he had them?" wondered Janice, speaking quietly.

Maria laughed. "I think you need to take the lead Sister. Father has the hots for a nun and you need to respond in a way that suits you."

"Advise me please, Maria. I need help now. This is all very new to me and I'm a little nervous."

"Well, your options are: rubbing his cock and masturbating him, known as a hand job; or you could suck him off, known as a blow job; or let him put his cock into your cunt and you let him fuck you. Or you could write, 'no thanks' on the pad and make sure he reads it."

Janice looked at Maria with a pleading face.

"If you turned your back on him, Maria, and I lifted your dressing gown and you bent over and I guided his erection into your pussy, he would be a happy man, I'm sure. Can we try that, Maria? Please? I'm a bit lost."

Maria looked at the worried Janice.

"Yes, let's see what we can do. I do enjoy Father Munro's cock and haven't had him for ages. Yes, we'll try that."

Maria turned around and bent forward over a bar stool and Janice lifted Maria's dressing gown right up and rested it on her shoulders. She looked at Maria's shapely legs and backside and smiled with appreciation. Then she put her hand between Maria's legs and whispered, "You are so beautiful, Maria."

"Oh, Sister Janice. Please keep me in after class and do whatever you want to do with me," whispered Maria in a mock schoolgirl voice.

Janice could not stop herself. Moving momentarily into the role of Maria's teacher was very exciting given Maria's response.

"I will, young lady. You can be assured of that. Now keep your hands away from your pussy until I can get to you."

Maria shuddered as the role-playing words from Janice found their mark.

"My God, Janice. You make role play more wonderful than the real thing. Can't wait to get more."

"Be quiet, child. Now! Try Father Munro's cock in the meantime. I promised him my sluttiest pupils pussy. Keep still, and when he yells, call out "yes Father" and "More please Father", in a loud voice." Janice's stern instructions made Maria utter a tiny scream.

"Sister Janice, you are priceless. I'm coming already."

Janice slowly dragged Father Munro onto his feet and turned him to face Maria's rear end. Then, still holding his cock, she nuzzled the end of it against the lovely woman's moist pink slit which nestled serenely in the midst of her profuse black pubic hair. Her cunt opened and Janice slipped the priest's cock into Maria.

It worked. Within moments, Father Munro was pounding Maria's vulva with gusto, yelling as he did, "There, Sister, take all of it. And make sure you come to the confessional during the week and I'll fuck you again. I know you love it."

"Yes, Father. Yes, I will! I love it. Give it to me harder, Father," Maria called out over her shoulder and in a voice loud enough for the priest to hear

Janice stood in front of Maria and the two smiled lovingly at each other. Janice had her hand up her skirt, then she lifted it and pulled her panties to her knees to let Maria see her playing with herself amidst her modest blonde curls.

Maria put out her arms and let her hands and fingers enjoy the feel of Janice's slowly rocking, mesmerising long legs, and her thighs.

Janice and Maria and Father Munro all came at the same time. The priest fell back down on his seat and the two women embraced and kissed each other.

"That was so good, Sister Janice," said a rather breathless Maria, sliding a hand over her very wet cunt.

"I thought so too, Maria. My sexual experiences are getting better every minute, thanks to you."

Maria picked up the notebook and wrote the word "Football?" and pushed it over to the now sleepy-looking priest.

"Yes, please!" called Father Munro as Maria straightened her dressing gown and headed back to the kitchen bench to put on more coffee.

Maria came over and took the priest's hand and led him through the doorway leading to a passageway that led to the sitting room and the giant television.

When she came back she looked at Janice and laughed.

"All men enjoy the simple pleasures of life, darling. Sex and football. And not always in that order."

It was late in the evening at Maude's housewarming party and Roger had manoeuvred the inebriated Angie back onto the garden seat and had pulled up her dress to cover her breasts. Angie held her panties in her hand.

"Thanks, lovely man. I do hope we meet again."

Angie attempted to stand but, whether it was the alcohol, or having just been shagged, she fell onto the grass. As Roger picked her up and put her back on the seat, he heard voices.

"Hello Roger. Fancy finding you here."

The smiling faces of Maria and Serina stared first at Roger and then at Angie. The two women had worked in the kitchen, helping mainly with cleaning pots and dishes. Now they were homeward bound.

"Hi Maria and hello Serina. Are you both going home, by any chance?"

"Yes, we've just finished and we're going home."

Both women were staring at Angie, noticing her slightly odd behaviour. Then they both looked at Roger and smiled.

"Got your hands full, Roger? Can we help?"

Roger smiled at his two tenants.

"This is Angela, but she prefers Angie. I've suggested that it would not be a good idea for her to drive home right now. I was thinking that she could rest up in that little front bedroom downstairs at my place, but I promised to go and check on Rosa's husband Bertie very soon. Is there any chance you two could take Angie home with you and put her to bed?"

Angie hiccuped for the umpteenth time as she stared at Maria and Serina.

"Lovely ladies, thanks for what you did before. That was beautiful."

Angie was mistakenly thinking these women were responsible for the recent licking and her orgasms, but which were really compliments of Janice as she passed by.

Roger laughed.

"It's all right. Mistaken identity. Can you help?"

Maria and Serina laughed loudly.

"It must have been good, whatever it was. Yes, we can help, can't we Serina?"

The mother and daughter looked knowingly at each other, which reminded Roger that he had every intention of fucking both of them, but probably not yet.

"Sure, Roger, we'll take Angie home for you. Don't worry about her. We might even take her to the cottage, where we can keep an eye on her. That way you won't have to deal with it early in the morning."

Roger thanked the pair, then turned to Angie and told her that the nice ladies had a bed made up at the house next door and she should go with them.

Angie giggled.

"I hope they give it to me like before."

As Roger began his walk back to the party, Maria and Serina took Angie's arms, lifted her up and began to walk her down the drive and to their house. Maria's voice came to him through the quiet night air.

"Now remind us, Angie? Tell us what we did to you before so that we can give it to you all over again."

Angie couldn't have been in better hands.

———

Roger's bisexual lover and soon to be the mother of his child, Caroline was home from London at last. She had rarely gone this length of time in the company of another person without speaking. Roger's tale of the two morning visitors to his bed, Maria and Serina, defied belief, but Caroline believed him.

"So I've told you at last, darling. You've been so busy up until now, and I didn't want to confuse you on Skype with my bed problems."

Caroline continued to stare at the man she had selected to father her child.

"I doubt there are many men who would call it a bed problem, Roger. Far from it. And I'm fascinated with your resolve not to acknowledge them in your bed. Some folk might even think that you had an even greater bed problem.

"Now! Your story has got me horny. Take me to bed please, darling. And if you want to fantasise that you are shagging Maria and Serina, that's okay with me. I will, too."

End

2

CATCH UP

EROS CRESCENT

No one on Eros Crescent remembers exactly the moment when the words COVID-19 or Corona virus were first uttered in their houses. Needless to say, it would first have been heard on a television report and the importance of the message would have taken a few days to sink in.

The world suddenly changed. Words and phrases like lockdown and self-isolation and social distancing were suddenly in the forefront of all conversations as people enacted the requests of government and the nation to act responsibly to assist in the national objective to achieve what quickly became known as flattening the curve.

For Roger, life couldn't have been less affected. His daily routines required only that he rose from his bed, showered and shaved, ate his breakfast, went for a walk, and made sure he had sufficient pens and paper. Although it did impinge on his new paying project.

He had been asked by Desley to write another booklet similar to the one he'd written for The Club, only this was to be for The Dunking, a venue he had not yet visited or, until now, even heard of.

When Desley explained the concept and related what the setting inside the warehouse was like, Roger was very keen to get started. But the arrival of the virus put an end to that project, at least until further notice.

For Caroline and Jackie and Miranda, staying at home was what they enjoyed anyway, that is when they weren't travelling abroad or window shopping or having coffee in cafe's.

All three women had worked in executive positions in London, but moving overseas brought that era to a close, although they had been invited to join similar companies in Australia.

A top of the range coffee making machine was promptly ordered along with a supply of fair trade East Timorese Maubisse, medium blend. Browsing online shops became the new window shopping.

Instagram took on a new importance as the pandemic took hold around the world. Stories and pictures of people in isolation doing amazing and sometime ridiculous things became the rage. Jackie uploaded hundreds of images of the inside and outside of the house, earning the praise of interior designers and architects.

Helen and her husband Frederico were effected in so far as Freddy's job as a flight controller at the airport was soon to be reduced in the number of hours he worked. However, there was no threat to his income as he was on standby as an essential service. But Helen's work as a freelance Human Resources consultant to industry came to a sudden halt. She embraced online conferencing on Zoom but this was no substitute for real hands-on consulting.

Helen was also restricted in her love life, already reduced as a result of her husbands responsibilities to Helen's two lovers who had inadvertently become pregnant to him.

Sophie and Freya now spent a night a fortnight with Freddy. Unable to visit or have visits from her own lovers, Polly or Celia Ashbee, Helen would just have to manage with her next-door neighbour, Mary. And what looked like the answer to maiden's prayer, The Club had been forced to close.

Mary's only loss of employment was her volunteer job at the Salvation Army Opportunity Shop which she would miss very much. She would also miss her sensual workout with her close friend Janice. But most of all, she would miss her newly found excitement at The Club which she had only recently opened.

Her niece and housemate, Sophie, worked at a horse stud and accepted reduced hours and looked forward to doing baby things at home. Because she and Mary lived next door to Helen and Freddy, the two households would have access to each other when needed. And of course, Freddy was to be the father of Sophie's as yet unborn child.

Alice and Frey both lamented the loss of work in their jobs as school counsellors. They both loved their jobs. Both were pregnant and accepted they would be forced to spend more time at home together.

Like most of the others, they had their favourite sex toys for when they weren't knitting baby clothes or doing jigsaw puzzles. And like so many women in lockdown, they visited female friendly porn sites online. The two decided that they would always share these internet session and happily parked themselves on the sofa, transmitting the websites from their phones to the giant television set via a magic little box. This meant that the images were so big that they felt they were in the same room and this proved most enjoyable on many occasions.

Bertie and Rosa were the older folk who were most vulnerable to the virus. They were happy to be isolated although Bertie complained that he would miss his fortnightly get together for coffee and cake with Freddy and Roger.

Bertie complained that he still had much to say on the subject of breaking down the worlds dependance on the "couples model" as he called it.

"Nothing good will happen while we maintain this ridiculous habit of pairing off for life." Firstly, in over half the cases, it doesn't work and people separated or divorced.

"Secondly, it was obvious that people who stayed in these relationships were deeply frustrated by the repressive demands on them of constantly answering to another person.

"Thirdly, paternity and property ownership where the only reasons this system was maintained and with the likely end of democracy as we know it looming, house prices and pension funds and equity investments were likely to collapse.

"And I haven't even mentioned the problems of religion and religious wars."

Rosa looked at him. She loved him dearly but managed always to call him out.

"You haven't mentioned love once."

"Sex and love are two seperate things, my dear. We both know that."

Most of the close friends and relatives knew that Rosa and Bertie had broken up many years ago and taken lovers. Rosa entered relationships with her close girl friends and occasionally, a man.

Sometime later, she and Bertie got back together as a couple, but both maintained their freedom to embark on other relationships if they so chose, and this arrangement worked very well. It wasn't that they were desperate to take on other romantic adventures, but just knowing that they were free to do so, made the difference. They broke up after almost twenty years and had now been together for nearly fifty years.

"It was a necessary pause," agreed the two of them, lovingly.

The two people that were originally going to be living together but in the end chose not too, were Edith and Jessica. But living at different ends of the same street meant that they would not need to forego their times together. And they, like Maude and the others living in number nineteen, had each other for company if and whenever they wanted.

Edith and Jessica had the boys on hand and could also still get a pizza delivered, although it sometimes took a little longer.

But then they learnt that they would now be sharing the boys with the very sexually active Maude and possibly with the two new girls who moved in to number eleven just before the lock down. Jessica and Edith's plans to invite the new girls in for a pizza, were in hand.

Edith still went for her walk on Mount Eros on most mornings where she usually met her friend Chloe and the two, more than not, would spend loving time together in Chloe's secret cave.

It was thanks to the lockdown, that Jessica met Chloe. Edith had long wanted the two to meet so when was Jessica unable to attend classes she accompanied Edith on her walks.

Jessica and Chloe were instantly friends. Both knew that the other understood Chloe's relationship with Edith. And when the rain fortuitously arrived on their first walk together, all three made haste to the hidden cave and it was only a few minutes before Jessica had Chloe underneath her on the carpet of leaves with Edith dragging first Jessica's then Chloe's shorts and panties off before sitting beside them with her bare breasts available for the occasional grope from both girls.

It was Desley who had the most to lose but she wasn't particularly put out. The Club had to close only two short months after opening and only a few weeks after Desley had formed a partnership with her friend Sally who had opened The Dunking venue. The Dunking was closed too.

Desley welcomed the opportunity to take a rest and review everything about the club and the new venture and be ready to make any necessary changes or recommendations to Sally when they eventually reopened.

She and her partner Alvie, lived on the premises. Alvie knew about Desley's dalliances with Roger who she said she also had a soft spot for.

Desley had laughed, saying that now that they had so much time on their hands, she would endeavour to entice Roger to pop in for a threesome if Alvie didn't mind sharing. To which Alvie replied that she wanted first go.

———

Maria and her daughter Serina were at first, forced to stay home with grandfather Aldo and the boarder, Giorgio. They mostly worked for older people as cooks and housekeepers in the stately home of Vaucluse and Woollahra.

They successfully applied for positions with the council as carers so that they could continue working.

They both had each other and the two live-in men to play with when they felt like it plus a range of toys they enjoyed.

———

Maud, the owner of the music school and owner of the property at nineteen Eros Crescent found isolation difficult, severely limiting her adventures although she had managed to entertain herself with young Ashton and Damian after the two became suddenly sexually aware after falling prey to pizza nights with Jessica and Edith.

And Sylvia and Stella, the two girl who she had enjoyed briefly when they stayed over on the night of her house warming party, seducing Maude with the help their bunny outfits, had booked in for music classes and accomodation the week before lockdown. Maud reasoned that maybe life wouldn't be too bad after all.

———

Peoples attitudes were changed in part by the arrival of the pandemic.

Australia was fortunate that it could close its borders and clamp down easily on travel.

Europe was badly affected and Britain failed in the early stages to take action which might have prevented many of the casualties they suffered.

The USA continued to be the sad case that it had slowly become.

Big enough to make loud noises but also it seemed, too big to be able to maintain good democratic government.

It was presided over by a man who couldn't cope with an enemy he couldn't see and he couldn't lash out at, or verbally deride.

The arrival of the invisible virus was to prove his undoing.

———

Life on Eros Crescent went on. The residents continued to love each other in many different ways and despite the sudden disruption of the pandemic, there was a feeling of optimism in the air.

Babies were on the way and new life called out for new ideas. And new ideas about how society worked were desperately needed.

Cross your sanitised fingers everyone, and hope.

———

The three volumes of the Eros Crescent series are available at Amazon Books as paperbacks or Kindle ebooks.

CONTACT

Publisher or review enquiries should include your full name and details in all correspondence.

Email address:
admin@richardlee.biz

RICHARD LEE PUBLISHING

Erotic Fiction

The Eros Crescent trilogy in separate volumes - as ebooks or paperbacks:

The Fifi Code

ISBN - 978-0-909431-02-0

Eros Crescent

ISBN - 978-0-909431-05-1

Mount Eros

ISBN - 978-0-909431-08-2

Excerpts from the Eros Crescent series - as ebooks or paperbacks:

Janice: A sexual enigma

Jessica: A young woman's journey

Helen: Enough is not enough

Maria: Always available

Mary: Catching up

The Club: Ladies love it!

Literary Fiction

Australian Short Stories

ISBN - 978-0-909431-00-6

Restless: A novel about two young men growing up
in Australia between 1900 and 1936 (Publication date not set.)

Out of Print Titles

Mathematics for Young Children by Helen Western
ISBN - 978-0-909431-01-3

Currajong: For Those Whom Schools Have Failed
by Bruce Wicking
ISBN - 978-0-909431-03-7

The Puppetry Handbook by Anita Sinclair
ISBN - 978-0-909431-04-4

Wordswork by Chris Davidson & Bruce Wicking
ISBN - 978-0-909431-06-8

Sheep Production by Murray Elliott
ISBN - 978-0-909431-07-5

Ducks for Starters: A Practical Guide to
Backyard Duck Keeping by Bruce Wicking
ISBN - 978-1-875207-00-8

Sweethearts by Colin Talbot
ISBN - 978-1-875207-02-2

www.ingramcontent.com/pod-product-compliance
Lightning Source LLC
Chambersburg PA
CBHW020651130626
46552CB00003B/1494